Special thanks to my dearest Ben, James, and Mom. To Angela, and her Mischevious Mess-Makers Oliver, Madeline, and Stella. To Kevin and his Merriment of Goofballs Clark and Carrie. To Andy and Alex for helping me find my way.

ISBN: 978-0-578-90563-1

Story by CarrieAnn Reda
Illustrations by CarrieAnn Reda
Edited by Benjamin Truitt &
James Herlihy

Might Fly
Art & Illustration

Things
that go
Bump

a compendium of the
common house monster

Introduction

There is a secret and magical world beneath our very feet, a world that has largely been ignored by naturalists: The lives and habits of the Common House Monster. Do not be misled by their name; these creatures are anything but common and they play a vital role in the ecosystem of human habitation.

I will never forget when I saw my first Common House Monster. I was just a girl and full of excitement but knew that I had to be still beneath my homemade monster viewing camouflage. I had created this makeshift monster blind from the instructions in my much beloved and well-worn copy of On Monsters: Their Behaviors, Habitats, and Diets by Percival St. George.

Beneath my hideout, my legs had fallen asleep and my eyes, trained on the plate of cookies I had left on the floor near the edge of my bed, had grown tired. When I had nearly given up hope, and was sure that my homemade cookies were not good enough, a small fuzzy hand reached out from under the bed and grabbed one. An Under-The-Bed Beastie, or Monsterous Domesticus Adorabili Underthebeddus, had made an appearance. Soon, the little fellow ventured all the way out from under the bed and made short work of the whole plate of cookies. Over the course of many days (and many plates of cookies), we developed a rapport. It was then that I became determined to become a monsterologist, and to study the lives of the Common House Monster. That same little Under-the-Bed Beastie (who I have named Fuzzball) has traveled with me and remains my friend.

During my many years studying monsters in the university and in the field as one St.George's students, I learned much about identifying and cataloging wild monsters, or Horribilis Monsterous. To my dismay, the Common House Monster was often overlooked. Interest in Monsterous Domesticus Adorabili was not only discouraged but looked down upon. The Monsterology community, and St. George especially, were completely dismissive viewing the Common House Monster as "not worthy of study." Percival St. George asserts in his addendum to The Complete Encyclopedia of Monsters entry on Monsterous Domesticus Adorabili:

"The Monsterous Domesticus Adorabili is a minor nuisance and pest to humans. There are too few species of interest for study in this area and most are only lesser variants of wild monsters. Indeed it would be a wasteful endeavor to spend more than a passing remark on one or two common monsters that have adapted themselves to household living."

This passage highlights the lack of interest and insight into the world of the Common House Monster and the micro-ecosystems they inhabit among the Monsterology community. It is my theory that each home is, in truth, its own fascinating ecosystem where no two House Monsters are alike. An ecosystem where, as my research shows, the Common House Monster plays an important role:

Keeping our homes free of Horribilis Monsterous. So, I have made it my mission to shed much needed light on the Common House Monster, beginning with my controversial doctoral thesis "Dust Bunnies and Couch Potatoes: Coincidence or Symbiotic Relationship."

My work would not be possible without exposure to the highly controversial theories of monster evolution proposed by Sir Nigel Biscuitbottom. I had the great fortune of meeting Sir Biscuitbottom while pursuing my studies. He and Percival St.George had their now famous debate on whether wild monsters develop behaviors that modify their forms that they teach to future generations, or if monsters actually evolve and new species arise through natural selection. At first, I was skeptical of Sir Biscuitbottom's arguments, but upon reading On The Origin of Monsters, I was persuaded by his studies of wild melancholic monsters and his theory that Melancholius Horribilis Monsterous, Goofballs and Giggles all evolved from a common ancestor. As Biscuitbottom writes in On the Origin of Monsters:

"In my findings, the melancholic monster, despite its great difference from Goofballs and Giggles in both appearance and behavior, clearly share many characteristics, especially the unique ability to effect a change in the mood of humans around them. It is possible then, nay, likely, that they share a common ancestor and nature has selected for each in their unique niche."

This compendium seeks to remedy the lack of awareness of the Common House Monster, and documents my observations in the field. My research has so far indicated that each home is an ecosystem in and of itself and that House Monsters do have an important role in the human world. I have lived among the House Monsters, learned their ways, and hope to share with you their many personalities and quirks so that you may grow to appreciate them as I do.

Fuzzy Tickle Monster
Monsterous Domesticus Adorabili Pes Ticklus

The Fuzzy Tickle Monster is sometimes called the Fuzzy Yellow Monster, but this is misleading as they come in all colors, yellow is simply the dominant variant. Fuzzy Tickle Monster is definitely not a misnomer though, as they have the interesting habit of using their fuzzy tails to gather toe lint from humans in the homes these monsters inhabit. They will, in fact, gather any sort of lint, but toe lint seems to be the most prized. What they do with the lint is rather curious. I watched them gather the lint into smooth little balls, which they exchanged amongst each other, as well as other House Monsters, in what appears to be a friendship display.

The Fuzzy Tickle Monster is crepuscular and they wait until someone is asleep (or almost asleep) to use their brushy tails to quickly gather lint, causing a slight tickle. They will gather lint not only from the humans of the house, but pets as well. In an experiment, I presented a gift of belly button lint (a rare treat) to one of the little fellows and this caused a lot of excitement as they treat lint from the belly button with great reverence.

Drip Drop
Monsterous Domesticus Adorabili Drippius

Drip Drops are highly social monsters who gather in large groups known as Puddles. They are crepuscular and gather in the evening and early mornings to perform elaborate dances that show off their tails. I observed that their singing and dancing is what creates the dripping sounds that give them their names. Besides their vocalizations, Drip Drops have special suction cups on their toes that they use to produce noises. Humans will often mistake the sound of Puddle gatherings for leaks. If a home has both Drip Drops and Fuzzy Tickle Monsters, it can make falling asleep quite a hassle.

Drip Drop Puddles will scatter when a human comes to investigate and will go back to dancing and singing once the human is tucked back into bed. It was a long time before I had gained their trust, but with persistence, a disguise, and the help of Fuzzball, my Under-The-Bed Beastie friend, they allowed me to watch and even participate in their dances. (They were not impressed by my attempt to mimic their dance. More practice is needed if I want to join the next Puddle...)

Shoe Borrower
Monsterous Domesticus Adorabili Fur Calceus

If your shoes tend to travel about the house, seeming never to be in the place you leave them, then the Show Borrower is probably the culprit. These fuzzy little monsters are looking for a nice warm place to nap and, for reasons that are still unknown to me, they prefer shoes. I was able to observe the Shoe Borrower's behavior by putting on my shoes, briskly running in place to get them nice and warm, leaving them out, and retreating to my monster blind. Soon, a Shoe Borrower came out of the shadows and rolled happily around in my shoe before dragging it away. Then, another Shoe Borrower came for my other shoe and carried it off in the opposite direction.

The Shoe Borrower's Latin name actually means "shoe thief", but this is unduly harsh in my opinion. The Shoe Borrower's discoverer, my good friend Lady Wordstrom, has a great deal of these creatures in her home and has had to wear mismatched shoes for her entire life. In my observations, a Shoe Borrower has no intention of stealing the shoe, but, they also have no intention of putting it back where they found it.

Pilferer
Monsterous Domesticus Adorabili Pilferous

The Pilferer is a creature of peculiar habits. In my field research, I found that they gather items that seem, to them at least, to be abandoned. In order to observe the activity of the Pilferers, I set up a bowl full of pens, pencils, and shiny buttons and waited patiently for days. Finally, a Pilferer made an appearance, making tentative steps out of the shadows and towards the bowl. Curiously, the Pilferer did not just simply take off with a few items, but closely examined the contents, picking and choosing what he wanted carefully.

Over the course of weeks I observed him and kept replenishing the bowl. Most curiously, if I replenished the bowl with the same items the Pilferer took the day before, he would run off and return with the item he took, placing it back in the bowl. This is why, when you lose something, you always seem to find what you lost right after you buy a replacement. This, unfortunately, leaves a home that is host to Pilferers with an abundance of items that never seem to be around when you need them.

Pfeffernusse
Monsterous Domesticus Adorabili Crustulum

These monsters are the reason that you will find empty containers of cookies and treats in the pantry when you could have sworn there was a precious one left over for your midnight snack. Pfeffernussen (plural of Pfeffernusse) are cautious nocturnal monsters that will travel from house to house scavenging (or so they think) "unwanted" cookies and candies, but keep their nests in one home. With an offering of freshly baked brownies, I was able to make the Pfeffernussen my friends and they readily accepted my presence among them. I was frustrated in my efforts to follow the Pfeffernussen on their nightly travels, and my neighbors are still put out about my research methods.

Pfeffernussen do not seem to be aware that the spoils they gather will be missed, and showed off their nightly gatherings to me with pride. It is my theory that Pfeffernussen actually play an important role in the home as their gathering behaviour lessens the likelihood that you will get ants. Because a leftover cookie, sitting all alone in its package in the cupboard, is how you get ants.

Blue-Striped Bandit
Monsterous Domesticus Adorabili Furrus

The Blue-Striped Bandit cannot resist the siren call of shiny things, especially if they are blue shiny things, making this monster very easy to observe. By putting out a few shiny blue marbles, I was able to develop a rapport with the Blue-Striped Bandit inhabiting my home. In my observations, their habit of gathering is instinctual and they seem to not be able to help themselves. Once a Blue-Striped Bandit spots a shiny, they must touch the shiny, then they quickly move it to a place with other shinies they have collected.

The Blue-Striped Bandit will have gatherings of shinies throughout the home and garden and not just simply at their nest. In order to understand this behavior, I set up my monster blind in the garden and watched one of my Bandit's collections, which was set up to catch the light and cast reflections. After many hours, a wild muck monster made an appearance and was repelled by the light and colors of the Bandit's display. It is my theory that this gathering behavior is one of several that protects the home from intrusions by wild monsters.

Dust Bunny
Monsterous Domesticus Adorabili Lepus

Dust Bunnies can be found in any room in the house, and they tend to gather their fluffy little selves wherever dust accumulates. Dust Bunnies are rarely solitary and gather in groups referred to as Puffs. They comb through accumulated dust for crumbs and other such treasures. Because the Dust Bunny is all covered in dust, monsterologists have mistakenly believed for years that Dust Bunnies are made of dust. My observations have shown this to be a faulty assumption. While they indeed are covered in dust, they are not, in actuality, composed of dust.

Unlike other house monsters, there seems to be no limit to the size a Dust Bunny can reach or how large in number a Puff can be. The only limiting factor is the cleaning ritual of the household they are living in (see my doctoral thesis for more on this) and whether the home has pets or children that are correlated with larger Dust Bunnies, and larger Puffs. The broom is the Dust Bunny's natural enemy and they will scatter whenever one is present.

Under-The-Bed Beastie
Monsterous Domesticus Adorabili Underthebeddus

No house monster is more maligned than the poor Under-The-Bed Beastie, and no creature could be less of a beast. They are shy but friendly monsters once you gain their trust, and, as with many other monsters, the key to starting a friendship is cookies. Lots of cookies. Under-The-Bed Beasties make tidy and cozy nests of fuzz and dust, which they like to decorate with the myriad forgotten things that make their way under the bed. Under-The-Bed Beasties share their home peacefully with other house monsters, mostly Dust Bunnies.

Occasionally, an Under-The-Bed Beastie will mistakenly scoop up a very put out Dust Bunny and place them in the nest, only to have the Dust Bunny pop out and walk away in a huff back to his Puff. Fuzzball (my Under-The-Bed Beastie Friend) has made an amusing habit of attempting to use Dust Bunnies as decor, Fuzzball behaves as though this is an innocent mistake (but I suspect he just has made a game of it). Under-The-Bed Beasties protect their nest areas and help keep the home free of the dreaded wild under-monsters, providing an important service to the humans they cohabitate with.

Yellow-Bellied Sock Muncher
Monsterous Domesticus Adorabili Flavo Ventri Soccus

Many innocent housekeepers have been blamed for the feeding habits of the Yellow-Bellied Sock Muncher who, well before your socks are washed, have snuck into the laundry basket and eaten the left one. It took many weeks of observation and experimentation to appreciate the Yellow-Bellied Sock Munchers foraging behaviors. I left out clean socks, socks worn for one day, and socks worn for two days, and they eschewed the clean socks for the dirtier ones (the smellier the better). I noticed that they preferred the left sock over the right one. In the name of research, I tried, myself, to taste a difference between the left and right sock and discovered that some things should remain a mystery.

The Yellow-Bellied Sock Muncher is yellow all over, but get their name for the little tummy dance they do after devouring an innocent sock where they make the yellow fur on their bellies brighter by rubbing it. They are quite proud of their tummies and show them off whenever they can. It is my theory that the yellow tummy displays, much like the Blue-Striped Bandits collections of shinies, deter wild shadow munchers from nesting in the home.

Spotted Tangle Monster
Monsterous Domesticus Adorabili Tanglus

As Dust Bunnies abhor a broom, Spotted Tangle Monsters can not abide by neatly coiled cords, strings, and anything else that is not sufficiently knotted and twisted. The Spotted Tangle Monster is something of an artist and uses the sundry cords and ropes they find to create elaborate nests full of their own peculiar beauty. In order to gain further insight into their habits I left out an especially neatly coiled cord and waited in my Monster Blind for a Spotted Tangle Monster to show up. I did not have to wait long. A little fellow came out of hiding almost immediately and went to work creating an artistic knot out of the cord I left while singing a little song to himself.

The Spotted Tangle Monster uses the knots they create to establish a territorial boundary. This keeps at bay wild tangle monsters who work with brambles, prickly thorns, and, if you are unlucky enough, your hair. My good friend Lady Wordstrom, having no Spotted Tanglers in her home, spends three hours every day untangling her hair thanks to the wild tangle monsters that sneak in at night.

Mischievous Mess-Maker
Monsterous Quasi-Domesticus Adorabili Wreccum

The Mischievous Mess-Maker evolved alongside human habitation, and is unlike other Common House Monsters. It has even been argued by Percival St. George that the Mischievous Mess-Maker is truly a wild monster as evidence to support his theory that Common House Monsters are simply pests and not a different species. The Mischievous Mess-Maker has therefore been labeled as quasi-domesticus.

Mischievous Mess-Makers are the reason that once glitter is introduced into the home it will never, ever, ever, go away. These monsters are drawn to small things that they can run about with and toss into the air. They sing and dance triumphantly with one another as they do so.

In order to better observe these habits, I lured them out with a large jar of glitter and months later still find bits of sparkle in my hair, on the floor, in the laundry, and in my dinners. The Mess-Maker celebration I encouraged was excessive, and in their glee, they scooped up innocent Dust Bunnies and doused them with glitter. The Dust Bunnies have still not forgiven me.

Garden Keeper
Monsterous Domesticus Adorabili Horticulus

Garden Keepers are very kind and gentle monsters that live outside the home in safe warm burrows, which are guarded from wild monsters by the shiny collections gathered by Blue-Striped Bandits and the territorial boundaries established by Moss Monsters. Because of their burrows and long floppy ears, Garden Keepers are often mistaken for rabbits.

Garden Keepers have a love of anything that grows and sing to the plants in the garden to encourage them to grow. Snails, lady bugs, butterflies, birds, and other garden creatures all benefit from the Garden Keeper's work. I watched these gentle monsters in the early morning as the Garden Keepers made their rounds placing drops of dew on the tips of leaves and flowers, all while singing their beautiful lilting song. Wild monsters seem to retreat from the song of the Garden Keepers, and it is my theory that these monsters are important guardians of the home. Garden Keepers have a special liking for dandelions and dandelion puffs, which is the reason they are so abundant in the garden and on lawns.

Moss Monster

Monsterous Domesticus Adorabili Mossius

Moss Monsters are the largest of the domestic house monsters and rival the size of many wild monsters. It seems this would make them easy to spot, but the Moss Monster has an excellent camouflage of green growing things and is often mistaken for a small hill. Moss Monsters have a symbiotic relationship with Garden Keepers whom they depend on to keep the miniature gardens that grow down their backs green and healthy. By holding still and keeping very quiet, as Moss Monsters move very slowly, I was able to observe the Moss Monster's ritual of visiting the Garden Keepers for greenery maintenance.

While, generally, a Moss Monster will stay on the periphery of the garden, leisurely patrolling the edge of the domestic territory, they do like to make their way onto rooftops to gather in sun or rain and take a nice nap. The Moss Monster's camouflage will change according to the environment. In desert ecosystems, for example, the Moss Monster can be observed mossless and covered in cacti and pebbles.

Giggle
Monsterous Domesticus Adorabili Gigglus

If you have ever developed a serious case of the giggles, you may be playing host to this Common House Monster. The presence of a Giggle will cause moments of unexpected levity making this monster particularly hard to study. A Giggle will rarely travel alone and a group of Giggles is called a Hilarity. If a wild melancholic monster invades your home, a Hilarity often assembles, which any Goofballs near will join, and chase the wild monster away. Sir Nigel Biscuitbottom theorizes that Giggles are closely related to Goofballs and that they share a common ancestor with melancholic monsters.

Giggles' habits are a mystery and poor Lady Wordstrom's estate is infested with them. When I came over to study them, I made sure to bring along an image of a very sad puppy to help me stay focused, but this ended up making it worse. Despite our best efforts, Lady Wordstrom and I could not explain what was so funny, and you'd have to have been there to understand why we spent the whole day giggling uncontrollably while looking for our shoes.

Goofball
Monsterous Domesticus Adorabili Goofus

Where there are Giggles there are also often Goofballs, a peculiar little monster that causes silly and fun behavior in those close to them. Much like the Giggle, studying Goofballs is difficult. You may think you have set up a proper experiment only to end up dancing ballet while pulling silly faces. (Not that I would know anything about that.) A group of Goofballs is called a Merriment.

While they will join in with Giggles to chase off wild melancholic monsters, they also play a valuable role in keeping wild boredom monsters out of the home. Boredom monsters will run from a Merriment, thus improving the mood of the household immediately even if the resulting silliness makes it hard to get work done. It is not yet clear as to how the Goofball, or any monster for that matter, changes the mood of those around them and further research into this area is needed. Nigel Biscuitbottom has theorized they are attracted to goofy behavior and recommends observing the goofball by making funny faces in the mirror and trying not to laugh.

Grumble
Monsterous Domesticus Adorabili Grumblus

The Grumble is a monster that you can find in any room in the house plodding around looking for crumbs and other treasures that can be found on the floor. Nearly invisible, you won't notice them going about their business until you trip or stub your toe on seemingly nothing. That "nothing" is in fact, a Grumble. When tripped over, a Grumble makes a low complaining sound that gives them their name, and scurries off to hide and pout. They are also quite put out by brooms, especially with rough bristles. It seems that their activity and calls help to warn Dust Bunny Puffs to scatter because a broom is on the way.

Grumbles love to gather round where people are eating and cooking in the hopes that a delicious snack will fall to the ground, and my poor friend Lady Wordstrom is frequently tripped in her kitchen (though this may also be in part due to wearing two different shoes when she cooks.) In my studies, I could not definitively determine whether or not Grumbles trip people purposefully so that food will fall to the ground, as Percival St. George argues, or whether they are just absent-minded wanderers.

Glob
Monsterous Domesticus Adorabili Globbus

While most other Common Monsters do not care for brooms, mops, and the like, the Glob loves a freshly cleaned surface and sees their presence as cause for celebration. In order to study Globs, I would scrub the floor of my research area until it was shining. As soon as I retreated to my monster blind, a group of globs (called a Gloop) descended onto the clean floor luxuriating in its pristiness.

Unfortunately for any house keeper, Globs, while otherwise harmless, are sticky and slimy. Their celebratory dances do not only make a mess of one's nice clean floor, but also attract the attention of Mischievous Mess-Makers. Once the floor is dirty, Globs lose interest and go about other important business, like leaving mysterious gross spots for you to stick your hand in. St. George suggests that the Glob, like wild muck monsters (See his volume on muck monsters Of Things Gross to Icky: Muck monsters in their natural environment), see clean spots as an invitation to establish a new territory where there are no other muck monsters as evidenced by the lack of grimy spots and footprints

Pubble
Monsterous Domesticus Adorabili Pubblius

The Pubble is a friendly monster who just loves to hug things that are soft, often creating wrinkles and whatnot in various household items. They unfortunately have a penchant for toilet paper, which is a favored nest building material, and this can lead to, shall we say, awkward situations. Pubbles also love fuzzy socks and will leave you stuck in the bathroom with cold feet.

In order to observe the Pubble's behavior up close, I left a selection of warm soft things in front of my monster blind. I waited a long time but eventually a Pubble appeared. She hugged each thing in turn and then seemed to think for a long while, doing a bit of a dance as she mulled things over. Finally, the Pubble settled on an especially fuzzy sock, hugged it and put it aside, then hugged all the other things again before running off with her prize (it is possible many innocent Yellow-Bellied-Sock Munchers have been blamed for the behavior of Pubbles). The Pubble's benefit to the home is undetermined at this point, but she's the reason that it is important to put the toilet paper on the holder to secure it from being pilfered by a Pubble.

George
Monsterous Domesticus Adorabili Amicus

Intimidating at first, as they are only a little smaller than the average Moss Monster, Georges are actually very gentle and friendly creatures. They have developed the strange habit of randomly picking up and hugging other monsters while uttering a call that sounds like "Geeorge", which is how they got their name. If you have a George in your home, you are very lucky as they protect closets, attics, and basements from intrusion by wild monsters. Who are not at all fond of big, long, and fuzzy hugs.

I had spent a long time trying to see a George for myself with no luck and then, one day (while I was dressed in a Dust Bunny disguise), one scooped me up while uttering an enthusiastic "GEE-oorge". He then put me down with a pat on the head and went off to other business. Lady Wordstrom has several Georges in her home and gets hugged many times a day. Her tangled hair and non-stop giggling leads them to think she's a house monster when she's looking for her shoes in the closet. She doesn't always think so, but she is very lucky to have such a rich monster ecosystem in her home.

44

Conclusion

The monster ecosystem in everyone's abode is different. When I visit the homes of my colleagues and friends, I'm amazed at the diversity of domestic monsters that are out there. From the great Georges in all of Lady Wordstroms disorganized closets, to the Hilarities, Gloops, and Puffs that roam about Sir Biscuitbottom's library, every home works like an island and the Common House monsters within it fill important niches. Unlike wild monsters, domestic monsters are highly adaptive whether you live in a big home or a small one. They find a way to flourish in any environment and that's what makes them so fascinating to study.

The work started here only scratches the surface of the amazing world of monsters for anyone young or old to explore. So, make yourself a monster blind or a decoy suit and a nice batch of cookies, and find out what mysteries you can uncover in your little world. Perhaps, one day, you'll be as famous as Percival St. George for his field work, as talked about as Nigel Biscuitbottom for his groundbreaking theoretical studies, or as happy as Lady Wordstrom as she laughs and walks unsteadily around her house getting hugged without warning.

CPSIA information can be obtained
at www.ICGtesting.com
Printed in the USA
LVHW070004010621
688993LV00003B/10

* 9 7 8 0 5 7 8 9 0 5 6 3 1 *